INSPIRING TRUE STORIES BOOK FOR 9 YEAR OLD GIRLS!

I am 9 and Amazing

Inspiring True Stories of Courage, Self-Esteem, Self-Love, and self-Confidence

Paula Collins

Table of Contents

Introduction

Hello! Do you realize how amazing you are?

You are exceptional. You are completely unique. Always remember that! You are the only you there is in the entire world, and that's out of billions of people!

The world has many big and small hurdles in store for you. Sometimes you might think that you can't make it. You might get very scared or doubt yourself. However, I want to tell you a secret. Everybody feels like this from time to time! Even adults.

In this Inspiring Stories book, you will meet other amazing girls. These girls overcome their fears, show great inner strength, and reveal their bravery.

Of course, you can show all these qualities too, but you must start believing in yourself. That is exactly what this book will help you learn to do.

You can shine your light in your corner of the world and bring that light to other people when you let go of fear and keep learning lessons. When you believe in yourself, you can accomplish anything. You are an Amazing girl

The Neighbor Needs Help

Have you seen that there are people who need help? Have you discovered how much you can do for someone with a little effort on your part?

The best way to help someone else is to surprise them by being kind, so you show them you care and make a difference. That's what this story is all about.

Marie was working on a puzzle of a beautiful macaw, she was looking through all the multicolored

feathered pieces to find the one that went in that space, she was a little frustrated but at the same time she was enjoying putting the sections together.

She heard something outside and looked out the window. It was Mrs. Emily who was on her way home, someone too old to walk with great effort with a cane, she had something on her leg and this made it difficult for her to walk, later she would know that it was a splint, apparently, she had had an accident.

He put down the puzzle and decided to go find out what was going on.

-Dad

-Tell me, daughter.

-Mrs. Emily walks with a cane and has something on her leg.

-That's too bad. Let's go see her, maybe she needs our help.

Marie liked the idea of going to see what was wrong with the lady. She liked how her father liked to help others and was kind. She shook his hand and they walked outside in the direction of the lady's house.

They knocked on the door and the lady opened it a couple of minutes later.

-Hello, John. -She said, - How can I help you?

-My daughter saw you arrive just now. We came to see how you were doing.

-Oh, how nice of you. Please come in.

The woman sat down. Her leg was hurting.

-What happened to her? -Marie asked.

-I was going out to buy fruit for the week and I slipped on the corner, my foot bent. It didn't break, but they put this on it so it will heal, I have a crack. Thank goodness it didn't break because at this age the bones don't weld the same.

Marie didn't think it was lucky at all, she thought it was a bad thing. She agreed that at least the lady hadn't had a broken bone.

-That's too bad.

-Not so bad, in a few weeks you'll see me bouncing and happy. I'll be good again.

-How are you going to do your things? -His father asked.

-I think I'll ask the boy on the corner to come and help me, the errand boy. I'll have to pay him, but no way.

They visited her for a while longer and then went home. That night while they were all at the dinner table, Marie talked about Mrs. Emily and asked about her family, if she didn't have anyone to come and take care of her, children or siblings. Her father told her that she was single, never married and now alone in the world.

-I wish I could help her, Marie said.

-What a good heart you have, said her father.

The subject remained there, but late at night, while she was with her father solving the macaw puzzle, Marie said to him as she placed a piece, I know how we can help the girl.

-I know how we can help Mrs. Emily. We can do some things to her house so that she doesn't go from one place to another.

-How would you do it?

-Surely the doctor asked her not to walk so much, so we can help her with house chores so she can rest and be calm.

-I like the idea.

They both spent a long time thinking about what they could do to help the lady, going to check things at home, she cleaning and they agreed that they would bring her food, the mom said that now she would make the meals for one more plate and so they would bring her every meal.

-Today when we were there, I realized that there were several things to do. - Said the father.

-I saw the house a little dirty, I could sweep and mop.

-Yes, there must be something to do and we can help.

Marie's father felt very proud of his daughter for what he had proposed, he realized that he had inherited her good heart. They agreed that the next day he would propose to Mrs. Emily the help they were going to offer her.

Before closing the bedroom door to go to sleep, he said to her:

-I feel very proud of you, of that desire to help others, I congratulate you daughter.

Marie felt good and went to sleep with a very gratifying feeling in her chest.

The next day, they went and proposed to Mrs. Emily to help and after she said no, because she felt sorry to bother them, she agreed, recognizing that she could use a hand. The father began to check the house, changed some light bulbs, fixed some wires that were about to short out, in the bathroom he fixed some dripping faucets, checked a clogged pipe and fixed a humidity that had a white stain on a wall.

Marie cleaned the house thoroughly, dusted the dust, fed and pampered a Siamese cat she had, combed it and removed all the dead hairs.

He cleaned the gutters that had a lot of leaves and were causing internal leakage when it rained.

Mrs. Emily apparently felt at ease with the presence, because she went to take a nap, and father and daughter laughed when the lady snored and seemed to be at ease. Since they were both free, they decided to play hide and seek for a while. They had a lot of fun.

After checking everything inside, including eating at Mrs. Emily's table, when Marie's mother brought the food, they went out to check the plants in the yard, to prune the lawn a little and to cut some branches of an old tree that threatened to crush the roof of the house.

Marie would never forget the look on Mrs. Emily's face when she woke up and saw her house, with all the repairs done and outside clean, with the lawn flush and the plants cared for, she was impressed how young, strong hands had accomplished so much. Marie and her dad were tired from the day's work but happy.

-Thank you, it's been a long time since I've seen my house as beautiful as it is today. Everything is beautiful, thank you, thank you.

-It's an honor, we want it to get better soon, said Marie.

-Thank you for your help, princess.

The lady wiped her tears. She was moved, and she felt loved and supported.

Marie could not stand it and hugged her neighbor and gave her a kiss on the cheek.

-We just wanted to help you feel better.

-I feel much better, even my leg hurts less. Thank you.

The next few days the support was visits, some small chores, and lunch every hour.

Then Mrs. Emily said that she could cook for herself and that she had improved a lot.

For about a week, they didn't hear from her. One day there was a knock at the door. Marie opened the door and saw Mrs. Emily without crutches, and she looked younger than before, refreshed. She had something in her hands. It was a chocolate cake.

-Thank you! -Marie said to her.

-Thank you for the help. You have given me these days. More than feeling sick, I felt sad and lonely because I had to do everything by myself.

Mrs. Emily looked very happy and grateful, with a deep affection and thankfulness that came from the bottom of her heart. The three of them ate cake and tasted coffee and tea.

No matter how old you are or what you do, a simple

gesture can brighten someone else's life. You can't imagine the needs that others have. Don't be afraid to help.

Every idea you have put into action, just like Marie proposed to help the neighbor and made her convalescence more bearable, you can mark help with others. You have a special gift in this world, and only you can share it. It is time. Be kind, and help others feel amazing and you will feel amazing yourself.

Messages of Encouragement

Has someone said something nice to you, and you feel better? When you are sick or sad, they say words of love, and you feel a little relieved. This is a story where you show that words can help you feel better or the opposite.

Mia had a couple of friends on the same block who had been together since they were very little, their parents would get together, and since they were babies, they would play; then they grew up, learned to communicate with words, and today, at 7 and a half years old, they are the best friends in the world. They are always included in any plan. If the fair comes to town, the three of them have to go or, failing that, the three families go; if there is something where they live, the three of them participate, even if they study in the same classroom, so they do their homework together and when they play in a group, who is a group? Exactly, them.

Olivia and Val were the other two friends, and although they always got along well, there were times when Olivia showed a strong personality and argued with them.

One day, when the three of them were playing at home, they made plans to play with stuffed animals. When they combined that, Val took out a toy kitchen, and in a few minutes, they set up a restaurant for stuffed animals. Olivia, who was the one with the idea, got first in line with her Rabbit, a pink stuffed animal she had had for a long time.

Mia had a stuffed cat and started arguing for her to get in line.

-My Rabbit is very hungry, said Olivia.

-My cat, too, gets in the back, don't be a cheater.

-I'm already here. Next time.

They both started to argue, pushed each other, and at the end, Olivia said:

-You're a bad girl. I don't want you anymore!

She left the room, slammed the door, and went home.

-Are you all right? -Val asked her.

-Sometimes it bothers me when Olivia says mean things to us, said Mia.

-Yes, she's hurtful with words; she's said a lot of things to me.

-I'm sure when she calms down, she'll come to apologize, but anyway, what she said leaves a mark.

-I understand you. I hope she will soon change his ways.

That same night Olivia appeared in the room, her chin was low, and her eyes were big and sad. She looked at the two of them with an air of guilt.

-You were right, she said to Mia; it was your turn. I

should have stood in line. I did things wrong twice. I said ugly things to you.

-Don't worry, I forgive you, said Olivia, but try to work on not hurting others with your words.

They forgave each other and continued playing. Olivia behaved well and did not abuse her friends, and apparently, what had been said was forgotten.

The next day, Mia's mother gave her daughter some news:

-Olivia's mother called me.

-Okay, where are we going? - Mia said because that was always the beginning of her mother's plans, "Val's mom called me, and we're going to the movies," or "Olivia's mom called me, and we're going to the beach for the weekend."

-Sorry, it's not a trip. Olivia is sick; she spent the night with a stomach ache and was vomiting this morning. The doctor saw her, and apparently, it was from something she had eaten. She reacted and is sick.

-Can we visit her?

-Sure, I'll ask her mom.

Mia thought about what she could do to help her friend, what to bring to encourage her to feel better, and how to motivate her. Finally, she spent the day chewing over an idea that might work and also taught Olivia a lesson about how words have an influence.

She decided to create a letter for her, decorated it with everything beautiful she had in her room, put glitter on it, made drawings with markers, made a bunny similar to her stuffed animal, and inside, she wrote a message:

"You are the best friend in the world and the prettiest; get well soon to play a lot."

That night, when they went to visit her, she gave it to her, they had never been that kind of details, so it seemed strange to Olivia when she read the message, her eyes watered and she said it was the nicest thing she had given her.

-Nice words fill the heart, get well soon, Mia told her.

-Yes, and hurtful words leave scars; I understood the message. Thank you, my friend. You make me feel better.

They continued sharing that night, and almost when

Mia was about to leave, Olivia had a great idea:

-What if we created a card company with positive messages?

-What are you talking about?

Did Olivia explain that why not dedicate themselves to bringing lovely messages to people in need?

Mia loved the idea, and soon Val was on board.

So, with no plans to make money, they began writing letters with positive messages to their neighbors, one to their parents to thank them for the effort they made every day.

Val's grandmother got sick, and they wrote her something positive to help her feel better.

A neighbor had surgery, and a letter was sent to the hospital with one of the family members telling her that they hoped she would come home soon and get better.

A neighbor lost his pet because it was already a very old dog, and they gave him a card with an identical dog with white wings on its back. The man hugged them and thanked them, saying that it had been the most beautiful gift they had given him in his life.

Thus, in a few weeks, they had delivered many cards with messages full of love for people, for the sad ones, the ones who had lost someone important, the sick, and even congratulations, like the one given to Olivia's father when he found a job in a company he had always wanted as a career goal.

"Congratulations on your new job, you deserve it; I'm sure you'll give it your all," and they put her father working at a computer.

One day, Olivia got sick with a very strong viral flu. She infected Mia and also Val; the three friends saw each other by video call, and they had to stay in bed and take all their medicines. They were sad, with little spirit to do anything.

What a surprise it would be when the mother of each one brought a large letter, the size of a notebook, the cover of each one had a favorite pet and many drawings, rabbits, kittens, and a puppy, inside there were many messages with different letters.

There were many messages from the neighbors and friends they had helped with their letters. Now they wrote them messages asking them to get better soon, to take care of themselves, and that they missed them. The three of them cried with happiness when they had those messages full of love in their hands; they realized that words could heal and make them feel better.

Olivia understood that she could fight with her friends, as it is part of human relationships. Still, she never said hurtful things to them again. The three always had paper and a marker to write messages of encouragement to whoever needed it.

Words have power, you can use them for good or evil, and if you give messages of encouragement, you can change someone else's day.

Be careful what you say and try not to hurt others with your words, there are things you can say that will hurt others, and you decide if you say it to fill them with joy.

The Broken Vase

Are there objects in your family that seem ancient to you and tell you stories of relatives you never knew? Do you take care of those pieces as if they were the most valuable treasure in the world? What would happen if something were to end up with that object? If you use your imagination, surely despite the circumstances, you can make new family memories about each other's pieces.

Laura was looking at the vase next to the fireplace in

the house. She was lying on a sofa in one of those moments when you don't want to do anything. Bored, she began to contemplate each place, and her eyes fell on the piece that seemed to have been in the house all her life because, apparently, her grandfather's father brought it when he escaped from who knows what country because of a war situation that she doesn't remember how it happened. Everyone wanted the vase because, apparently, it was the only thing great-grandfather had brought with him.

Laura saw her two brothers, who were just a few meters away from her. The younger one was fighting with the other one about something in the car game they had. It was something to do with some buildings and that the street they had entered was in the opposite direction.

Their tempers were getting hotter, and they were fighting more intensely. Their mother would peek through the door and authoritatively ask them to calm down, or they would go to bed.

Although their mother appeared from time to time to bring order, it seemed that the two of them were getting cranky as the minutes went by.

-Thomas and Johnny, if they keep up that fight, they're really going to go to sleep.

-I'm sorry, mom, said Thomas, who was the oldest, but Johnny doesn't want to listen; you can't go through here.

-Let him go, don't worry about it, don't forget that they are playing.

Thomas raised his eyes to the sky. Laura rolled her eyes; she couldn't stand those fights. She took the cell phone and started to see things, a way to get away from the fight between the two of them.

Somewhere in her brain, she heard that the kids seemed to be fighting more, things moved, and soon there was a loud CRASH where the world seemed to stop.

Laura looked away from the phone and saw in the direction of her brothers, who looked frozen. They didn't move a muscle, and a terrified grimace was directed at her sister as if asking, "Did we do it?" Surely Laura's now terrified look also confirmed to them that they had indeed made a grave mistake. They had broken the vase with so much affectionate value.

-What did they do? -Laura said almost in a whisper.

-It was an accident.

-Dad is going to be furious.

Her siblings, who, second before, had been fighting for a long time, now trembled and looked in the direction of the door where their parents would surely appear at any moment since the cracking sound when the vase broke had been loud.

-Although it had been a vase brought by the great-grandfather, he was called

grandfather in the family, which is very bad.

Laura put down the phone and went to look at the pieces; almost everything had been destroyed, except for a piece that was in the center of what was the ornament, egg-shaped and dark blue.

-Can you explain to me what is going on here? -It was the mother who had appeared in the doorway and seemed to be processing everything her eyes were seeing.

-It was an accident, Mom.

She didn't have time to answer, as the father appeared in the doorway as well.

-What was it that creaked? What broke? -The father was silent for a moment and then added, The vase! Who did it?

The two brothers looked at each other, and Thomas spoke.

-It was us. We were playing, and...

-Don't say any more. -Said the father.

He approached Laura: He had a strange expression, he took her by the arm firmly, but without squeezing her, he took her to the door and told her: Please, take your brothers to the room and stay there for a while. We have to clean this well and avoid leaving pieces on the floor to hurt the soles of our feet.

Laura nodded and motioned to her siblings, who seemed relieved to get out of there.

-Is Dad going to punish us? -Thomas asked his sister.

-I don't think so; he would have done it already. But he asked us to stay here.

-We didn't mean to, said John.

-I know, they were playing. It was an accident.

John had a little runny nose. Laura thought she would have to entertain them and make sure they didn't do anything wrong.

-Shall we play a game? -She suggested.

-I don't want to, said John, Dad will come to scold us right now.

-Yes, sure, said Thomas, who seemed to be thinking about the consequences too.

-We should have thought about what we could break, said John.

-And I should have at least given them a look and not neglect them and let them end up like that.

-Don't feel bad, said Laura. I think we can do something to make up for what happened, do you think we can try to create something?

-What do you have in mind? - said Thomas.

-I'll do anything.

-I think they'll like the idea.

Laura thought about how the vase was already ruined, except for the piece she was holding; the rest was safely in the trash by now. But something could be done to create new memories so that later this day would be the beginning of a new chapter in the family history.

-We can take the poster board, that nice one we have and never use at school, and create a nice mural with each of us on it.

-What is that? -Thomas asked.

-An art like those we see in the streets that people make with spray paint; remember the other day you saw one of a cat?

-Ah! I like it. Shall we make a cat?

-Well, it's not what I thought, but something like that for mom and dad to get that gesture from us.

The two brothers got excited, and their heads started flying with ideas. Thomas took out the cardboard, John looked for the pot with brushes and colors, and Laura took out the tempera paints and acrylics. In a couple of minutes, they had a whole workshop set up to start making art.

The first thing Laura did was to take the piece that had been left over from the vase; she took the school glue and smeared it all over the back, then she placed the piece on the middle of the cardboard and left it there very still until it would stick.

The two brothers began to paint. They decided to make a family story, the two of them playing with one's hand on the other's shoulder, showing that they were a family that loved each other no matter what. At the top, Laura made the back silhouette of her mom and dad, hugging, who seemed to be contemplating them. From the center of the piece of vase, she made some white streaks that seemed to be a light coming out of it and covering everyone as if showing that despite the circumstances, that memory would always be present.

-What are they doing? -asked the mother, who appeared in the room.

The siblings looked at each other with frightened faces; Laura was the one who answered.

-We are making a new family mural.

-Oh, but that's beautiful what you've done!

-Will you help us? -John said in a sweet voice.

-Of course, I will. -Mom said and sat down with everyone.

Soon Dad appeared and saw what was going on. It didn't take him long to understand the meaning, and he sat down with everyone. Each one contributed ideas, and they reinforced the play.

Two days later, without saying anything to anyone, Dad took the work they had done, and in the afternoon, returned with it in a very nice frame. Now, on the fireplace rested that painting made from love, which started from an accident.

Accidents happen, they are part of life, and we cannot always escape them. The family had known how to take advantage of the children's idea of creating a new object in something that symbolized a family moment.

If we make mistakes or something breaks, it is normal to feel sad about it, but it is not a bad thing to die for because you can take advantage of it and, from the pieces, create a new opportunity that can be even more beautiful than it was before. Besides, it is an opportunity to strengthen ties.

Brave as a Bear

There are situations in life that force us to be brave. Whether it's going to the doctor or riding a bike, being brave means you stand up for yourself and aren't afraid of anything. In this story, you will see Annie's bravery put to the test. True bravery lies within us, all it takes is a little push, and you'll be just like Annie when she went camping.

Today is an exciting day, Annie and her class is going

on a field trip! Annie has been excited for some time to go camping, and now the day has finally arrived. She packed her bag, said goodbye to her mom and dad, got in the bus car, and sat down next to her friend Carly to head to school.

"Are you ready for camp?" Annie asks.

"Yes, I am; why are you so excited? Carly asked.

They were many things Annie was excited about, like walking in the woods, roasting marshmallows, telling camp stories, or scavenger hunts! The list was long, but overall, Annie was very excited to spend a few days outdoors, just like when she went camping with her dad.

Annie looked out the window as they arrived at school; upon arrival, she went to her classroom and stood at attention to answer when her roll was called.

"Here!" she said when she heard her name, the teacher crossed her off the list, and so did the rest of the class as they waited for the bus to take them on the field trip. She could hardly contain her excitement!

When the bus arrived, Annie and her classmates

excitedly loaded their bags onto the bus.

On the trip, Annie sat next to Carly, chatting and laughing with joy.

On the way, they played spy games and riddles to pass the time.

After a while, Annie exclaimed, "I see the camp!" pointing out the window.

All the companions were happy when they reached the camp.

There were many trees and plants everywhere. Annie and her class would soon learn a lot from them.

"I can hardly wait; what will we go do first?" wondered Carly.

All the children got off the bus and were greeted by the camp guide, Marco.

Marco would be the one in charge of assigning bunk beds and would take them on adventures in the woods.

"I hope everyone is as excited as I am," Marco said.

He divided the class into boys and girls and allowed them to settle into their bunks. Annie sat on her bed and began writing in her journal about this adventure before Marco pointed out to them that they would soon be walking down a trail.

"I can't wait!" said Annie and got ready to line up to leave. Annie received a list of all the items required to complete the treasure hunt and was confident that she would be able to complete the tasks successfully.

Marco led the children down the trail, and Annie listened to all the sounds of nature, like birds chirping, owls hooting, and the wind rustling in the bushes; she was already having so much fun and couldn't wait to see what was next.

"I found an acorn," Annie said and stuffed it into her bag. She found many of her items, but as the class continued down the trail, Annie stopped when she saw another path she wanted to go down.

She knew she shouldn't go too far, but she was very tempted to try something new.

"I don't think they'll mind," Annie thought and broke away from her group, finding more items like rocks, pinecones, and shells.

"I'm almost done," Annie thought and crossed off her list of what she was getting. She continued to wander down the path with curiosity.

When Annie had already advanced along the new path, she realized that she might have made a mistake. She couldn't remember how to get back on the right path. She was so far from her classroom that she couldn't ask for help.

"I have the compass that my dad gave me to find my way," Annie said and reached into her pocket to pull it out.

With the help of the compass, Annie kept walking and went deeper into the forest, looking for the way back. The sun was already setting, and Annie needed to get back to her class, but suddenly, she heard a rustling sound coming from behind a tree.

She wanted to investigate, so she approached the mysterious noise when suddenly, from behind the bushes, a bear appeared!

Annie froze in fear; the bear approached and began to sniff her. She had never encountered a bear before and didn't know what to do. Annie stood still while the bear looked at her curiously. She tried to scream for help, but no one heard her, and she only succeeded in making the bear more interested in her.

"I can't be bear food!" Annie thought to herself, and at that moment, a brilliant idea occurred to her.

She remembered that she was carrying some candy in her pocket that her mom had given her when she said goodbye to her wishing her good luck.

She took the candies and slowly showed them to the bear to sniff; when she managed to get his attention, she threw them as far as she could, making the bear go after them. Annie ran as fast as she could to get out of the bear's sight and managed to escape. Once she felt safe, she tried to find her way back to where her companions were supposed to be...

"Where are they?" said Annie looking in all directions until she heard her friends in the distance and ran to join them.

The classmates were relieved to see Annie coming; they were very worried because they could not manage to find her; they surrounded her to greet her and to ask her where she had been.

"I'm so glad to have found you; I thought I was lost forever!" Annie said.

"I ran into a big bear, and I thought he was going to eat me," she continued, "until I was able to distract him by throwing some candy I had in my pocket, and I managed to run away," she said.

"Annie, that's why we shouldn't stray from the path, this one is safe, but in the forest, some bears have been spotted that I'm sure you wouldn't want to encounter; it could be dangerous. You could have been badly hurt," said Marco.

Listening to Annie's story, her classmates applauded her in admiration, and Marco was very proud of her for having been so brave.

"What you did was very smart, you kept your cool, and with your bravery, you managed to get to safety," said Marco.

When they returned to camp, they lit the campfire, told stories, and roasted marshmallows. Annie and Carly sat together in the warmth of the fire.

"I'm so glad you're okay, Annie," Carly hugged her.

"Me too, it was really scary, and I almost didn't know what to do," Annie put her marshmallow on the fire.

"Attention, everyone. We have a very special award

to present at this time," Marco said.

"We will present this award to someone for fearless and smart."

"Annie, today you are being awarded for your bravery. You faced a bear and were able to protect yourself, and that takes a lot of courage to do that," Marco presented Annie with the bravery medal as an award.

"Wow, I can't believe it. I've never won a bravery award before. I can't wait to show it to my parents," Annie said and hugged the award tightly. This means so much to me!

At the end of the night, everyone went back to their bunks, and Annie wrote everything down in her journal and told the story of how she managed to trick the bear. Her classmates were amazed and admired Annie for her bravery. Annie was as brave as a bear.

Being brave is about being fearless and taking on challenges, just like Annie. She was scared and lost and fought off a bear, all because she didn't back down and showed true bravery.

We can all show courage every day by trying new

things and never backing down, no matter what anyone says or how we feel.

When you find the roar inside you, you will be strong and not afraid of anything.

Irresponsible Skateboarder

Do your parents ask you not to do things, and you feel it is unfair? Do they warn you of the dangers you may encounter along the way? This is a story that shows how disobeying the rules can have serious consequences.

Julia loved skateboards; when it was her birthday, she asked months in advance for that to be her present. She was begging to receive it and to be able to start playing with her friend Sally around the

blocks from home.

She was lucky enough to receive it and told her neighbor to go and play. She seemed to have been born for it; she skated perfectly, did not fall, and moved smoothly from one side to the other, breaking without any problem.

Soon she was already doing some pirouettes and lifting her off the front.

She had a few falls, but they were not serious.

Julia's father was loving to please her in whatever she asked, but he also had a temper and always asked her how to do things or to protect herself so that nothing would happen to her. If he forbade her to do something, she had to comply and beware of breaking that rule because there would be consequences with punishments of weeks.

Julia didn't like it when her father gave her that look. She was the one who demanded order, that the room was nice, that she bathed and brushed on time, that she did her homework on time and all that she didn't like sometimes. Now he looked at her sternly, as if waiting for a response from her for doing something he didn't know if it was wrong or not.

-I think I told you that you could play in this whole area, along the front of the blind street, not go out on the main road, let alone look out over the slope. - He said.

-But Sally and I have barely looked out. Besides, we are careful not to go down there.

-But you were so close, I saw you, inches away from the slope; one carelessness and you would go down that slope and who knows what would happen, you would fall, break a bone, or worse... get hit by a car below.

-But we won't do it.

-You have to abide by that rule, or I'm confiscating your skateboard until further notice.

The father entered the house after giving the warning, and Julia saw Sally.

-Dad forbids me to do everything. He always controls me. I can't stand a lot of things sometimes.

The father seemed to hear what Julia said because he came back.

Sally, to avoid witnessing more trouble, began to

skate, came around the hill and did a pirouette, and came back with speed.

-You see, dad, Sally does all that without a problem. She doesn't even fall.

-She's not my daughter. You are; when I ask you not to do it, I know why I'm saying it; it's not a whim. I'm protecting you. I had put up with buying you the skateboard because I didn't want anything to happen to you, and your friend lives in a flat area with more space. We have that slope there that I'm afraid might cause something to happen to you.

The father asked her to get off the skateboard and took her inside, grounded for three weeks. It was a harsh measure, but it was his way of educating and telling her how to do things.

After this punishment, she was able to go out with Sally, her father was out with friends, and her mother was taking a nap. It was the perfect time to have fun with the skateboard.

She did more pirouettes than ever, jumped over mounds, moved around, jumped over some benches, and managed it quite fluently. Julia felt free to be doing some flips that would surely have made her father jump to confiscate the thing again.

-What if we went down the slope? -said Sally mischievously.

-But my dad...

-He's not here, come on.

Julia knew that facing that danger was one thing, but facing it was quite another, so she thought about it for a moment and finally decided to accept, to take the plunge.

The first one to do it was Sally, who stood on the skateboard and, with one foot, propelled herself. When she reached the slope, she put herself on top, in a position to keep her balance, and descended at great speed. When she approached the part where the cars passed, she turned easily and stopped on a small ramp; from there, she pointed with her finger that everything was fine.

Julia thought about everything again. Her father was gone, her mother was asleep, and it was now or never that she could face that temptation that always called her. Surely nothing would happen if she was a great skater.

She started down the hill, the skateboard vibrated under her feet, she picked up more and more speed, and the air hit her face. It felt great, fear, adrenaline, danger, breaking the rules.

Sally seemed to scream but didn't hear. She tried to make the turn but didn't turn, and she kept going straight ahead. Tires screeched, she lost her balance, and Julia ran over the car and fell on the hood. She was looking straight at the passenger seat, and there, her father looked scared.

Julia's father got out of the car and rushed her off the hood, and put her on the sidewalk to check that she was okay. He was extremely scared. He began to check her back, her sides, her legs, and her neck and asked her to move her limbs to confirm that she was okay.

When he saw that she was fine, beyond the scare and the fact that she had fallen like a sack on the hood, nothing had happened to her, he carried her in his arms to the house, pushed her as he walked up the hill, but not once did she complain.

Once at the door, he stood Julia up and firmly took her by the hand. Her father had never reprimanded her with violence, he knew of children who were spanked, and he imagined that having broken this rule meant that for the first time, they would learn it.

Her father's silence, the way he looked at her and moved, made her think so.

Her father, who had his eyes wide open, far from starting to scold her, told her in a voice broken with tears:

-Daughter, you could have died. Do you realize how close you came to having suffered a serious accident?

Then he hugged her and held her for a long time like that while he seemed to be thankful that it hadn't happened.

The skateboard was confiscated until further notice, until she showed that she could be trusted. Although Julia promised never to break the rules again, she realized that her father was right. He just wanted to take care of her and loved her very much.

Finally, much later, when she was able to play on the skateboard again, she was at least 50 meters away from the hill, and when she was going to get close to that area, she would get off, pick up the skateboard, and walk away, then climb back on.

When she wanted to play on wider terrain, she would go with his father to a park where she could more safely practice other tricks.

Parents make rules that may seem annoying to you, but they only do it to take care of you and protect you, don't break them because something bad can happen to you.

Susana the Perfectionist

How does it make you feel when you make mistakes? Do you feel bad? Do you say mean things to yourself?

Mistakes come in all shapes, and forms and you have to know that they are amazing, even if it surprises you to know it. Because you can learn from them. Mistakes are the path to success and improvement.

Susanna woke up before her alarm went off. She

felt happy and excited about the day ahead of her. She had a routine every morning to get her things done before leaving for school.

When the alarm went off, Susana settled herself to start getting ready for school. She turned off the alarm, and the morning silence reigned throughout the house.

She stretched every muscle in her body and slowly got out of bed.

She felt a push of adrenaline to get out of bed. It was the best way to start the day.

She made her bed just as her mother had instructed. She went to school that day and felt that everything had gone just as she had timed it with exact minutes so that nothing would go wrong. She was very methodical.

Mistakes didn't go well for her, she felt she couldn't, and that's why she was so exact in her things.

When class was over, she would pack up her things and leave everything very organized to go home.

Her friend Vanessa appeared next to her and told her something about the game on Friday, that they

would have to arrive a little earlier.

-No way -Susanna said-. She already had everything planned. She would have to check again, so she opened her bag and started scribbling that Friday's time was changing at practice.

The bell rang for the second time announcing that everyone had to leave now, and for Susana, it was a sign that she had to go. So, she got ready and ran out as soon as she had finished planning the message Vanessa had given her.

When she left, she went straight home, she had the minutes counted to arrive on time and do her things without missing anything.

Having Vanessa make her rewrite things in the diary she had already saved didn't sit well with her. It was wasting valuable minutes. She would have to manage that better in the future.

Once at home, she began to take everything out of her suitcase, arranging it with millimetric care, but soon she began to worry because something happened that altered, or rather, ruined the day in a catastrophic way for her.

A math notebook was missing, in which she had

written down the homework she had to do and hand in the following day.

-I can't have left that notebook behind- she said.

She had never left a notebook behind, and as she took things out of her bag again and again, hoping to find it, she felt deep down that she would not see it again that day.

She thought of Vanessa that by interrupting her, she had made her forget that notebook. If she had at least waited for her to finish putting it away, it wouldn't have stayed with her. She felt anger and frustration and clenched her fists. She couldn't believe she had made such a serious mistake.

She told herself that she would never have forgotten the notebook if she hadn't been interrupted.

This incident had put her in a very bad mood. She went into the room and slammed it shut.

-Who is that walking around the house like a giant and knocking down doors? -Said her father, who appeared in her room.

She was upset, so she was not afraid to show what

she felt and let her father know.

-I'm really mad at Vanessa for leaving my math notebook on my seat, and now I won't be able to turn in an assignment tomorrow.

The father looked at her with a hint of sadness and, at the same time, with a smile.

-What a problem.

-Yes - said Susanna – now, I don't know what I'm going to do; tomorrow's whole day is ruined for me.

She distracted me at the end of the class to tell me that they had changed the training time on Friday and that's why she stayed with me because she was putting things in her backpack.

Her father was someone who was in a good mood, so he knew that what his daughter was feeling, while she had a right to be angry, was misplaced.

-Honey, that sounds to me like you're the one who made a mistake.

Susana looked at her father with annoyance; she couldn't believe what he had just said.

-What? -she said.

I think Vanessa was helping you. She warned you about a last-minute change, and you made the mistake of leaving the notebook. How would you have known about the change if she didn't tell you? Besides, she had no idea that you had everything timed at that moment when you put things away.

Susanna realized that her father was right, but instead of feeling relief, she now felt more anger.

-Mistake? -she said.

-Yes.

-Did I make a mistake?

-Yes.

She could not credit that she had made a mistake, for she could not remember when she had last done so.

As she analyzed all this, she began to worry more. She saw her father, and her features softened, more so when she noticed that he was looking at her with love. Her father reached over, put a hand on her shoulder, and stroked her head.

-Why are you so angry, daughter?

She answered with a cry and hugged him to unburden herself and tried to speak stammering.

-I made a mistake! -she said with an effort.

Her father let her unburden herself, and when she stopped crying, he hugged her and began to talk to her with much love: Daughter, it's okay to make mistakes because they are a good thing; you don't have to fear that because they give you the opportunity to think creatively and solve problems, and learn new things about yourself.

Susana did not say anything, but she was no longer crying. She wiped her tears.

-What does that mean?

-You're a wonderful girl, a very good student, and responsible, but you put a lot of pressure on yourself to be perfect as if you were a watch, and you don't have to be like that. Perfect is not good. It doesn't exist. You want to keep everything neat and tidy in a way that overwhelms you. Look at your younger sister, who has everything messy and doesn't have a pair of matching socks together.

Susanna laughed thinking about that. She couldn't bear to see how her sister could live like that.

-The fact that your sister is like that doesn't make her bad because she's doing well in school. Imperfect is not bad.

She thought of her younger sister, who yes, was messy, but she wasn't bad. Always kind and good at things, with talents.

Perfection doesn't mean that your life will be stress-free, but when you keep trying to be perfect, you miss moments where you can learn more about who you are and how you handle change; mistakes are great.

Susanna cried again at the thought of the mistake, but she was beginning to understand what her father wanted to tell her.

They gave each other a big hug, and he told her that he was thinking about how he could find a solution to the mistake.

-I forgot the notebook, but now that I think about it, I know what the teacher wants. I will be able to do it in another notebook or on a few sheets of paper and then at home, and I will put everything in the

notebook.

-You see, there is a solution, and there was no need to react that way. You see, it was easy, and if you hadn't forgotten that notebook, you wouldn't have had to think to find the solution. How do you feel?

-Great.

Susana started to do her homework and completed it in a while. That night in her bed, she wondered what it would be like if the next day, when she made her bed, she wasn't so radical in making it up or even leaving it unmade for a day.

When she woke up the next day she made the bed, it wasn't perfect, but she didn't care!

Susana knew that even if she made mistakes, she didn't have to be frustrated like that, but that she could take advantage of it and grow to be successful. She was already happy with that. She saw it as a learning experience.

Learn from mistakes and adversity, when you do, you can grow in many ways, and you will become more amazing than you already are. Every mistake is a lesson, don't forget that.

Trustworthy Person

Have you ever seen danger when no one else has? Have you come across places that could hurt you and tell others? Are you trustworthy? This is an adventure story where being observant and warning is part of teamwork.

Polly loved the vacations, times when she didn't have to take notebooks, beyond the review she did with her mom for a while each day, but there was no homework, uniforms, or getting up early. It was the

best time of the year after Christmas.

After lunch, a group of girls would get together to look for adventures. Since they lived in an area that had a rural setting, they could wander among the trees, cliffs, and small mountains they explored and see the birds, squirrels, and some wild animals grazing.

Polly enjoyed going with them, because each one had a talent, for example, Martina was good at climbing trees. Pamela was an expert at jumping over rocks and Laura had a keen ear for hearing movements in the bushes and warning of danger.

-Let's go, said Martina when Polly opened the door to her house.

-I'll throw the water in the backpack, and we'll go, said Polly cheerfully.

Pamela and Martina greeted her by raising their hands.

This day's excursion was important. They would climb a little higher than normal to a tree that everyone called Jobo. It was gigantic. Her mother said it was older than her grandfather. It was a fat tree, almost as wide as a car and as tall as a four- story house, with wide branches, full of many leaves and seeds as if it had pimples. It was a very old tree that had silently watched the city grow.

The plan was to go climbing. Martina had the plan to climb it and see the city. According to her, her brother had told her that from the top, you could see the whole city in its fullness, and she didn't want to miss that view. Although her plan was for everyone to climb, including Polly, Polly was afraid of heights and was looking for a way out so as not to go up.

The group of friends left Polly's house and made their way up the mountain. As soon as they left the small town, they had to cross a bridge, but the adventure was calling, and since it was summertime, the river that ran under it was low, barely a stream, and they all passed by betting on who would get to the other side first, over the stones, choosing the ones that were dry so as not to slip.

Although they were not exempt from injuries, sometimes they stumbled and scraped, but they shook it off, rubbed themselves a little, and continued the adventure.

Polly noticed that Martina was having more fun that day than ever. She looked excited.

-When I get to that old tree, I will climb it like I climb the stairs in my house to go to the second floor.

-I'll climb it when I get to my apartment with an elevator. -Pamela said.

-Yes, because the Jobo has an elevator. -Laura said.

They all laughed.

-What I mean is that I will climb it faster than all of you. Let's see, Polly, how are you going to climb it?

Polly, who the last thing she wanted to do was to climb, said with a smile:

-I'll climb it in one jump.

-Oh, she's worse, said Martina. Now she's jumping like a spring.

They all laughed and continued betting on who would climb it first.

As they climbed up the mountain, the tree that could be seen from the city here began to grow taller and taller, as if it were a giant guarding the whole area and sleeping, hoping not to be disturbed.

There was a moment where they all remained silent, the slope was steep, and also that tree seemed to create a shadow over the entire lack of mountain. Although none of them recognized it, they felt a little afraid for the adventure they had prepared.

Besides, Martina had said that the last one to arrive or the first one to chicken out was a rotten egg. None of them wanted to be.

-It looks like it's bigger than we were told, said Polly.

-Yes, it's going to be our big challenge, said Martina.

-Challenge for you. You'll climb it like a turtle. -Said Pamela.

-Challenge for you, who will see me from below with regret for not having reached the top. -said Laura.

Each one of them thought that she would get there first, well, all of them except Polly who, while she was climbing and breathing through her mouth because of the great effort it represented to climb, thought about how to save herself from not climbing that tree that every step made her look up more and more to contemplate the height.

Finally, the mountain stopped climbing, and they

reached a plain with a shadow that made it look like dusk, but in reality, it was the branches of the Jobo tree, so wide and abundant that they covered the sun. The tree was fatter than their parents told them, it was at least two cars wide and tall. They could not calculate it. It looked like a building.

The first branch was several meters high.

-Wow, it will be quite a challenge, - said Martina when she saw it up close. She slapped her hands as if to warm them up and approached.

Pamela took out some matted gloves she had to play with, which she said would help her not to get hurt. Laura spat on her hands to get a better grip, although she immediately felt disgusted.

-It's now, then. -Said Pamela, who started to climb, but began to slip. It was hard for her to do it.

-I'll get there first, said Laura, who jumped up and grabbed a bump. She pushed herself up, but she wasn't strong enough.

-This is mine, said Martina, who concentrated and began to climb.

With each movement, she fell into a bump or hole in

the tree, and soon after, she was a few meters off the ground. The others watched her from below, frightened and excited.

She reached the first branch.

-Everyone is a rotten egg, she shouted from above, excited.

She continued climbing, the others silently watching as she seemed to shrink as she climbed.

Polly noticed something strange on one of the branches and shouted:

-Beware! That branch is rotten. You're going to fall.

-It's nothing. It's nothing.

She continued climbing, and the branch creaked and broke. It was all a matter of a thousandth of a second. Martina fell a couple of meters, but in a reflex, she grabbed another branch and looked very scared. She almost fell.

This scare was enough for her to descend. When she reached the bottom, she said:

-I was going to reach the top, but as none of you

dared, I am the winner.

They were all so overwhelmed by the branch that no one took credit away from her.

They walked home down the mountain in silence.

On the way back, at one point, Martina came over and put her hand on Polly's shoulder and smiled at her as if to say "Thank you" for warning her. Polly felt that she had given her to understand that she was someone to trust and was attentive to the team.

After this incident, the next few adventures they took were less risky. The lesson helped them realize that they were human and could get hurt if they were not responsible in their games.

Polly continued to enjoy the vacations with her friends, going out to different places, they went fishing, they climbed but not very high, and from that day on, they saw the Jobo with respect. It was a tree that did not like to be disturbed.

Being part of a team implies being aware of what may happen, warning in time to help others, and sometimes reserving to take some risks, even when others want to do it.

Listen to that inner voice that tells you not to do it, and when you are in a group, warn others of what may be in the near future.

Discovering New Cultures

Have you ever imagined how many kilometers the world is? Billions? How do you think they live? Do you think they are like you or do their own things? This story shows how every culture is different and has its own ways of living.

Since Aura had arrived in that new country after traveling many hours on a plane where she felt like she had circled the planet 8 times, they finally landed.

She had already seen people everywhere, who spoke a little differently than her, who had a different way of being, the clothes, their faces, the way they even walked. She knew she was not at home, that it was a different culture.

Already at her cousins' house, where she had gone to spend some time, at her uncle's house, she had dinner in front of her; it was a plate with many vegetables on top, almost covering her head. Aura looked at them with fear.

Her cousin was next to her and looked at her strangely.

"What is this, Charlie?" She asked her cousin.

- "Food."

"Yes, but I haven't seen it, what is that yellow stuff?" She asked again.

"They are all vegetables, and if you try them, you will like them. We eat them a lot here."

Charlie couldn't stop looking at her with amusement.

" Since I came to this place, everything has been so... strange," Aura said.

"No, it's not weird. I think if I went to your country, the same thing would happen to me. It's called culture; we are all different." Her cousin told her very kindly.

Aura finally dared to take a piece of food and taste it, she did it with the one that seemed the strangest to her, expecting to find a bitter taste, but she opened her eyes and said:

"This tastes very good."

"Everything is delicious. Give yourself a chance to enjoy it."

She continued tasting other foods, the meat, the other vegetables, some she knew, and she felt that each one had a new flavor, and although one or another she didn't like so much, she still ate it; her mother had taught her not to leave anything on the plate.

Her aunt, along with her cousin, were the ones who had gone to pick her up at the airport. Her uncle had not gone because he was working, and they did not know each other, so there was a lot of expectation for how that first meeting would be. Aura went by asking what he was like if he seemed in a good mood, if he was someone affectionate.

Her cousin, who was fond of making jokes, told her that he was sullen, that he would get angry for nothing, and then told her the truth, that he was not, that he was loving and very playful.

As Aura had so many things on her mind, anything could happen, and she was afraid.

As time went by, she played with her cousin and talked to her parents by video call. In her country, it was already night, and where she was at that moment, there was still a very bright sun. That also seemed curious to her, as she had always heard that it did not get dark at the same time all over the world due to the movement of the planet, but living it was a totally different experience.

Finally, her uncle arrived, walked through the door, and stood looking at her.

"This is a lovely girl." Said the uncle, opening his arms and pulling her in to greet her.

Her uncle was a thin man dressed in a suit and had a big mustache covering his upper lip.

"Hello, uncle," she said as she ran to greet him.

He picked her up and pressed her against his chest

as he planted a kiss on her cheek.

Although he spoke Aura's language, he had a strange accent that she couldn't quite put her finger on. She found the way he spoke funny but said nothing.

Long before coming on this trip, Aura had seen that her aunt wore different clothes from her own. She noticed several pictures, and she especially liked the one with the purple and pink suit. It was beautiful and colorful. She had never seen anything like it, and she asked her mother why they dressed like that.

"It's the way they dress in their country. Don't you like it?" her mother said.

"Yes, I like these dresses, although I don't like my uncle's shirt. I think it's too flashy. Dad wears shirts with one color."

The mother laughed and told her they were a bit showy, but that's how they wore them there.

Now, in her uncle's and cousin's country, she stood before her aunt, who had a beautiful suit with gold lace and other flashy shades all over her garment, and her uncle, who, although dressed smartly, had a flashy shirt underneath.

What do you like to play in your country? Asked her uncle.

I play soccer a lot. I have some friends in my area where we have a lot of fun. I love it. She said.

I see. Do you want to play? asked her uncle

Aura agreed immediately.

The three of them went out to the backyard of the house, from somewhere they took out a big ball, like the professionals, and began to play, without any rules of the sport, simply playing to take it away from each other and scoring in a door that served as an archery.

They had a lot of fun in their games. They spent at least an hour until the uncle, already sweaty and tired, sat down and asked for a break.

"Go on, children, this old man can't go on any longer," he said.

The two children laughed and continued playing; this time, one shot, and the other tried to catch the ball.

When they were both tired too, they went into the house. The cousin's mother appeared with some brightly colored drinks that she said were from local fruit. For Aura, again, it was a challenge. Still, she remembered that her mother had told her that she had to try new things in that country and that whatever they gave her, even though she didn't know it, it would be a unique experience. She couldn't refuse it without trying it first.

She held her breath, took the first sip, and tasted it. She was surprised. It was sweet, she could not describe it, but it was like a mixture of watermelon for its refreshing, banana for its creaminess, and peach for its consistency. But it was more, it was as if she had mixed many fruits. She asked her aunt, but she said no, it was only one fruit, and that she would show it to her later.

"We have a present for you," said her uncle.

He motioned to his cousin's mother, and she went off into one of the rooms and soon after returned with a box that was wrapped in wrapping paper. If Aura had seen flashy things so far, this was the most attractive of all, very colorful with colors that, if you put them against the sun, would illuminate a whole street.

She began to uncover the gift, which had a red ribbon

with a beautiful bow on top. It was light, and she could not imagine what it could be. She unwrapped it while her uncle, aunt, and cousin watched expectantly for her reaction.

When she uncovered it, she found something that lit up her face. It was a finely folded piece of cloth. She touched it. It was very soft. It could almost slide through her fingers.

She took it out. It was a pink dress with golden lace at the corners of the sleeves and neck. She knew immediately that it would fit her perfectly as if she had been measured.

"Your mother told us that you liked some of my dresses," said her aunt.

Aura nodded.

"Our tailor-made one with the measurements your mother sent."

Aura remembered that weeks ago her mother had been going through a lot of her clothes, she knew she was preparing the surprise at that moment, she made a mental note that she would congratulate her.

She spent the vacation season learning new things,

open to enjoying every experience, and dressed as if she were just another local. She knew that giving herself the opportunity to learn about other cultures and respecting them was the way to nurture her experiences.

If you dare to enjoy each new culture, venture into worlds you have not seen before, respecting what each one has. You will enter a universe where you will come out more prepared and know that the world is different and rich in customs.

The Writer

Have you started chasing dreams and feel like they're too far away? Do you want to achieve something, and it doesn't work out the first time? You may not know it, but in order to achieve dreams, you have to work to achieve them. Patience is important and is the cornerstone.

Lori had a dream since she was a child, and it was to be a famous writer, where people would read the stories that flowed in her mind and made her fly through unimaginable worlds. Since she was a little girl, she has created stories and learned to read at a very young age. Everything that fell into her hands she devoured in a short time.

She had written some short stories and poems to her pets, her parents, and her grandmother. What she loved most was her collection of short stories that together made a great story.

Every day she saw her writings, she felt very happy. She was inspired and invented a new story.

One day she wanted to participate in a joint reading of great writers of the city. She wanted to be an inspiration for other children.

She asked her mother if she could participate and if she would buy him more notebooks and pencils.

Her mother told her that as soon as she left, she would go to the stationery store to get everything she had asked for.

Her mother showed up with a ream of paper and several notebooks, as well as many colored pencils. That day was one of the happiest. She went to her room and set up a small studio where she spent hours writing and thinking up stories. Although now that she had set up this studio, she was not so happy with her work, deep down, she believed she could write it better. Change verbs, eliminate adjectives, put more poetry in some sentences, and change outcomes.

She asked herself many questions about how to make her work better.

-If I want to be a famous writer, I have to learn how to be one.

She found a creative writing class at the local library and signed up to improve her writing. She saw that she was making many mistakes and worked to improve them. Over the next few days, she felt that her writing was getting better and better.

When she felt confident enough, she went to a literary café where the most famous writers of the city were present and wanted to apply to do a reading for everyone.

The woman who was attending smiled sweetly when she saw her:

-Thank you for visiting us, but sadly we are not accepting new writers now. Maybe you can come next year because we already have a full schedule.

Lori felt very sad, but this did nothing but push her to keep preparing. She went to more classes and worked. She even got more praise for her writing, and those who read her were overwhelmed by her solid stories and unforgettable characters.

The following year she went with another collection of writings for them to see. The woman who had served her last year was still there, and upon seeing her, she was surprised. She noticed that she had improvements in her writing, but sadly she turned her down with almost the exact words.

Lori could not believe it.

-Don't you like my writing? -she asked.

The woman came clean:

-Your work is excellent, but you can improve more. You just need to keep practicing. I'm not going to accept what you're proposing this time.

Lori went home disappointed, sat down in the living room, and looked at all the books she had been accumulating for years. She had been working on becoming a better writer for some time. She remembered each of the classes she had taken and remembered a pattern in everything:

Each of the writers there had been writing for years before they were recognized. As she read biographies of writers, she realized that many of them were rejected and had a hard time getting the place they had now.

Lori smiled a calmer smile and went back to writing. She continued to study and began to create a collection, a sort of little saga that flowed from her soul, the words flowing with a beauty she had never felt before.

When she was about to finish this work that she had decided to write on the computer, she inadvertently deleted one of the chapters, the one she considered to be one of the important ones

-It can't be! -she said regretfully.

She tried by all means to recover the file, she even went to a programmer, but he told her that there was nothing to be done. She had left work with a gap, the plot part, not the poetic or philosophical part that she had worked on in others.

Lori sat down to cry, heartbroken by what had happened. She worked so hard on creating these works, and now in such a foolish way, she had lost one of the best chapters.

Venting, she went back to the computer and rearranged things. The next day she sat down and reviewed each of the chapters, even the gap in the one she had missed, and discovered that she had achieved something abstract, that this missing chapter could leave scenes open to interpretation, and that they themselves represented an interesting... proposition.

When it was time to go to the famous literary café to knock on the door again, she did not feel so sure. She did not feel so sure because she expected the woman's rejection.

-It's good to see you again, said the woman when she saw her enter, I hope you surprise me this year as always.

-This year, I didn't want to bring loose writings or snippets of stories, but I was encouraged to bring a composition that was accidentally interesting.

-Well, let's read it, then.

Lori showed her the whole text, and the woman asked for time to read it calmly. She didn't want to leave but stayed browsing through the books. The woman went through the stories, finding interesting plots with twists she did not expect, philosophical phrases throughout the writing that she liked, reflective themes, and poetry in many lines. No doubt, it was the product of someone who had put effort into creating it.

-I feel something is missing here, the woman, an expert reader, told her.

Lori, with some embarrassment, told her what had happened.

-Well, although the gap is felt, I noticed it because I've read other things of yours, but a zero reader hasn't, and I love this missing because each reader can draw their interpretation. I'll be glad to have you here, reading with the other writers this year.

Lori felt like she was going to lose her heart from all the jumping she was doing, but she had made it. She and her parents celebrated with a dinner out, and she excitedly awaited the day when all the writers and people who came to the café to see writers would come to hear her readings and start rubbing elbows with other writers.

-We are very proud of you, said her parents.

-Are you proud because I wrote something good?

-Yes, but more so because you didn't give up despite rejections. You always stood up. You could have given up at any time, even with trouble on the way, but you showed love and patience, and now you have here the prize for the effort.

She went home happy that day and would soon enjoy a full house reading with people in awe of a young woman with such writing gifts.

Lori was in awe the day she saw everyone's impression as she brought her reading to a close. She was almost in tears as she watched everyone rise to their feet and give her a standing ovation. Usually, they did it out of formality or from their seats, but now they seemed truly immersed and moved by her story.

You should never give up on your dreams, even if many obstacles appear along the way. Lori didn't. She knew that it takes time to achieve your dreams.

It may take longer than expected to achieve your dreams, but you can get what you want, so don't be discouraged by the obstacles you encounter along the way. Keep building your craft, and soon you will be the best writer, painter, or whatever you want to be.

The Younger Sibling and the Contest

Have you ever had to make difficult decisions and don't know what to do? Sometimes we have to choose difficult things, and we must know how to do it correctly and choose the most important one. This story will teach you that.

Emma loved her brother very much, and wherever she went, she always went with him. She was the older sister, so she took care of him and made sure he had everything he needed. When he came home from school, she would bring him a treat, and they would play together, download apps on the phone, and play games.

They spent many hours together as their parents worked, so even though they were siblings, she sometimes acted as a little mom.

One thing Luca, her brother, had taken a liking to was bicycles. He had been given one for his birthday and had learned quickly. Soon the back wheels were off, and he was riding from one side to the other like an expert. This made Emma very proud, and she always told everyone.

Emma wanted to give the best to her brother. He was her great love, and so at the first call, he always came, and they played a lot. She was attentive to helping her parents to educate him like when he didn't want to eat, she sat next to him and made him eat everything, or if not, she made him forget about sweets.

One day they announced that a cycling competition was coming to town, and there was a section for children. Whoever participated and showed what they could do, there would be a gift just for participating. All to promote the sport to the children.

Emma was excited, she asked her parents for permission, and they said yes, to take him, as it would be a lot of fun for the child.

-Do you want to go to the bike contest?

-Where is it?

-Nearby, in the park.

-Can I take the bike?

-Of course! You're going to participate.

The boy started jumping up and down excitedly. He couldn't believe he would be in a bike contest. He had only seen it in videos on the internet.

-Before we go, we'll spend the next few days rehearsing so you can do well, even though you already do it the best. So, when we get there, you'll be the best, and everyone will see you. -Emma told him.

They spent the next few days practicing in the backyard. He would get on the bike and start jumping from one side to the other, he would go up a bank, move forward, and when he braked, he would turn the whole bike around, and in this way, he was preparing himself to be the best, they even watched videos on the internet to find new things to do.

It was amazing how Luca learned so easily on the bike.

In this way, they both seemed to get smarter every day. Even though Luca was the one who was going to participate, as a teacher, Emma helped him and gave him the best advice. They were both looking forward to participating.

Emma had also checked the bike, and on the internet, she found out what needed to be done in maintenance. She put air in the tires, prepared the brakes, and tightened screws and nuts so that nothing was out of place.

Then they would begin a routine they had both prepared. Emma told him how to warm up and prepare to move around the space with a circuit of various obstacles, and the plan was to overcome them in the shortest time possible and work hard on the ones where he still lacked experience.

Finally, they did an obstacle course on a single wheel.

Emma smiled and smiled that, in the end, she didn't even fall. Everything was perfect. She had learned very fast and felt like she was watching one of those live shows on the sports channel where the cyclists did pirouettes.

Everything looked great so far. They even rehearsed in the rain because they could not make excuses for anything.

The day before the show, they had already prepared the bag and everything they needed. Luca ate dinner and started sneezing.

Half an hour later, he had a fever.

-I don't think Luca is well, Mom, Emma told her.

Yes, I just saw him. I gave him some anti-allergic and his medicine to make him feel better. Did you get wet?

-It rained these days, but we changed our clothes.

-He caught a cold. You know they can't get wet. Let's hope he feels better tomorrow.

I hope so because we're going to the contest.

-If he wakes up with a fever, it's time to take him to the doctor.

-Mom! But the contest.

-Well, part of being a big sister is that sometimes we have to make decisions that, even though we don't like, we know it's the best thing to do.

-What do we do?

Emma thought about everything. On the one hand, they had spent much time on this contest. They wanted to show everyone how well he was doing on the bike, but if he woke up sick, they couldn't go to the competition because he could get worse because of the physical activity. Besides, Luca didn't look good. The truth was that he didn't even seem to be interested in this contest.

Emma did her mental math and knew what was best.

-Yes, Luca should go to the doctor to see him if he wakes up sick.

The next day the boy did indeed still have a fever. They went to the doctor first thing in the morning so that he could prescribe medicine that would cure him soon.

At home, Emma was in the room with her little brother, and they ate together. Then she sat on an armchair there, and they talked until he fell asleep. She didn't notice that he also fell asleep and spent the night in the room close to her brother.

The next day she woke up when she heard Luca shouting happily that he was feeling well and no more snot was coming out of his mouth. He was thirsty and hungry.

Emma remembered that this was the day of the contest and that the time to arrive had already passed.

She turned on the television and began to see the children doing the pirouettes and demonstrating their talent. Shortly after, they were each given a prize, a beautiful toy, one of those that appeared on television.

Emma spent some time thinking, and at the end, she said, You know, we don't need to show off:

-You know, we don't need to prove that you're the best on the bike. We both know you are.

Luca smiled and nodded happily.

Soon after, the mother looked at the boy to confirm how he was feeling and was relieved to see that he had healed.

-You look good. Those medicines healed you quickly.

The mother saw Emma and stood next to her, watching the TV screen. The children were still there, happy with their gifts.

I know how hard you worked for this contest. But I am proud that you put your little brother's health first, and it is the best decision you made. Someday you will be a wonderful mom just like you are an amazing sister today.

Her mother kissed her on the cheek.

-Thank you, Mom. I'm so glad I had your help, and besides, next year we'll get ready, and we won't get wet so we can go to the contest and win.

Luca also agreed. The three of them spent that day having fun and in the afternoon. They went out riding their bikes. They happily enjoyed themselves with other neighbors who had also gone to the contest.

They both took these training days as an experience where they had a lot of fun and also prepared themselves to be the best next year.

Emma knew that she had to take care of her loved ones and the people she loved, and although sometimes we have to sacrifice something we have worked for, the reason is for greater causes, even if it hurts. It is the right thing to do.

The moral is to take care of the people you love. They can be pets, friends, or family. Watch over them, and when they are sick is the time when they need you the most, stay by their side even if you have to sacrifice some things.

Made in the USA
Columbia, SC
27 May 2023

17399006R00052